My Own Little Bible

Is Presented To

_____

On

_____

By

_____

My Own Little BIBLE

New International Version

Illustrated by David Barnett

Chariot Books™
David C. Cook Publishing Co.

Published by Chariot Books™,
an imprint of David C. Cook Publishing Co.
David C. Cook Publishing Co., Elgin, Illinois 60120
David C. Cook Publishing Co., Weston, Ontario
Nova Distribution Ltd., Torquay, England

MY OWN LITTLE BIBLE
©1989. 1990, 1991 David C. Cook Publishing Co.

Illustrated by David Barnett
Flex cover Illustration by Kathy Wilburn
Cover and internal design by Kay Currie
Edited by Brian Reck

All rights reserved. Except for brief excerpts for review purposes,
no part of this book may be reproduced or used in any form
without written permission from the publisher.

Scripture quotations are taken from the Holy Bible, New
International Version, © 1973, 1978, 1984, International Bible
Society. Used by permission of Zondervan Bible Publishers

First Printing, 1991
Printed in the United States of America
95 94 93 92 91   5 4 3 2 1

Library of Congress Cataloging in Publication Data
Bible. English. New International. Selections. 1991.
    My Own Little Bible   p. cm.
    Summary: Presents selected texts from the Old and
New Testaments accompanied by illustrations.
ISBN 1-55513-682-6
I. Chariot Books. II. Title.
BS391.2 1991a
220.5'208—dc20   91-17581
                                              CIP
                                              AC

Thanks to the team that made this book possible:
Cathy Davis, Dawn Lauck, Randy Maid, Paul Mouw, Julie Smith

A Note to Grownups:

Reading the Bible can be one of the most important experiences in a young child's life.

The Bible teaches children important truths that they will carry with them for a lifetime. The Bible introduces children to the God who loves them so very much.

My Own Little Bible uses actual text from the New International Version. Children will accurately learn some of the world's most beloved stories—from the story of creation to Paul's missionary travels—direct from the Scriptures.

Children will love looking at the beautiful illustrations and want you to read the stories again and again.

TABLE OF CONTENTS
OLD TESTAMENT

God Made Everything	10
Adam and Eve Sin	12
Noah Obeys God	14
Abraham Waits for God's Answer	16
Jacob Tricks His Father	18
Joseph Forgives His Brothers	20
Miriam Saves Baby Moses	22
Crossing the Red Sea	24
God Gives Food	26
The Ten Commandments	28
Ruth Honors Naomi	30
Samuel Listens to God	32
God Chooses David	34
David and Goliath	36
Jonathan Helps David	38
God Guides Elijah	40
Elijah Goes to Heaven	42
A Servant Girl Helps Naaman	44
A Fiery Furnace	46
Daniel and the Lions	48
Jonah and the Big Fish	50

NEW TESTAMENT

Mary Hears a Promise	52
Wise Men Rejoice	54
Fishers of Men	56
The Lord's Prayer	58
Calming a Storm	60
Jesus Heals a Deaf Man	62
Jesus Is Our Best Friend	64
The Good Samaritan	66
Zacchaeus Is Sorry	68
Feeding 5,000	70
Lazarus Comes Back to Life	72
Jesus, The King and Savior	74
Jesus Says Good-Bye	76
Jesus Dies For Us	78
Mary and an Empty Tomb	80
Not Alone	82
Jesus Goes to Heaven	84
God Rescues Peter	86
A Miracle and a Mistake	88
Paul Helps a Church	90
John Writes About God's Love	92

God Made Everything

And God said,
"Let there be light," and there was light.
"Let there be an expanse between the waters to separate water from water.
"Let the water under the sky be gathered to one place, and let dry ground appear.
"Let the land produce vegetation. . . .
"Let there be lights in the expanse of the sky to separate the day from the night. . . .
"Let the water teem with living creatures, and let birds fly above the earth. . . .
"Let the land produce living creatures according to their kinds. . . .
"Let us make man in our image. . . ."

Genesis 1:3, 6, 9, 11, 14, 20, 24, 26
Value: Faith

Adam and Eve Sin

When the woman saw that the fruit of the tree was good for food and pleasing to the eye, and also desirable for gaining wisdom, she took some and ate it. She also gave some to her husband, who was with her, and he ate it. Then the eyes of both of them were opened, and they realized they were naked; so they sewed fig leaves together and made coverings for themselves.

So the LORD God banished him from the Garden of Eden to work the ground from which he had been taken.

Genesis 3:6, 7, 23
Value: Conviction

Noah Obeys God

So God said to Noah "... make yourself an ark of cypress wood.... I am going to bring floodwaters on the earth to destroy all life. ... But I will establish my covenant with you, and you will enter the ark—you and your sons and your wife and your sons' wives with you. You are to bring into the ark two of all living creatures, male and female, to keep them alive with you. Two of every kind of bird, of every kind of animal and of every kind of creature that moves along the ground will come to you to be kept alive."

Noah did everything just as God commanded him.

Genesis 6:13, 14, 17-20, 22
Value: Obedience

Abraham Waits for God's Answer

… he laughed and said to himself, "Will a son be born to a man a hundred years old? Will Sarah bear a child at the age of ninety?"

Now the LORD was gracious to Sarah as he had said, and the LORD did for Sarah what he had promised. Sarah became pregnant and bore a son to Abraham in his old age, at the very time God had promised him. Abraham gave the name Isaac to the son Sarah bore him.

Genesis 17:17; 21:1-3
Value: Patience

Jacob Tricks His Father

Rebekah said to her son Jacob, "Look, I overheard your father say to your brother Esau, 'Bring me some game and prepare me some tasty food to eat, so that I may give you my blessing in the presence of the LORD before I die.' Now, my son, listen carefully and do what I tell you: Go out to the flock and bring me two choice young goats, so I can prepare some tasty food for your father, just the way he likes it. Then take it to your father to eat, so that he may give you his blessing before he dies." Then Rebekah took the best clothes of Esau her older son, which she had in the house, and put them on her younger son Jacob. When Isaac caught the smell of [Jacob's] clothes, he blessed him. . . .

Genesis 27:6-10, 14, 15, 27b
Value: Honesty

Joseph Forgives His Brothers

Then Joseph said to his brothers, "Come close to me." When they had done so, he said, "I am your brother Joseph, the one you sold into Egypt! And now, do not be distressed and do not be angry with yourselves for selling me here, because it was to save lives that God sent me ahead of you. For two years now there has been famine in the land, and for the next five years there will not be plowing and reaping. But God sent me ahead of you to preserve for you a remnant on earth and to save your lives by a great deliverance."

Genesis 45:4-7
Value: Forgiveness

Miriam Saves Baby Moses

But when she could hide him no longer, she got a papyrus basket for him and coated it with tar and pitch. Then she placed the child in it and put it among the reeds along the bank of the Nile.

Then Pharaoh's daughter went down to the Nile to bathe, and her attendants were walking along the river bank. She saw the basket among the reeds and sent her slave girl to get it. She opened it and saw the baby. He was crying, and she felt sorry for him.

…She named him Moses, saying, "I drew him out of the water."

Exodus 2:3, 5, 6, 10
Value: Wisdom

Crossing the Red Sea

Then Moses stretched out his hand over the sea, and all that night the LORD drove the sea back with a strong east wind and turned it into dry land. The waters were divided, and the Israelites went through the sea on dry ground, with a wall of water on their right and on their left.
The Egyptians pursued them, and all Pharaoh's horses and chariots and horsemen followed them into the sea. Then the LORD said to Moses, "Stretch out your hand over the sea so that the waters may flow back over the Egyptians and their chariots and horsemen."

Exodus 14:21-23, 26
Value: Courage

God Gives Food

…"At twilight you will eat meat, and in the morning you will be filled with bread. Then you will know that I am the LORD your God."

That evening quail came and covered the camp, and in the morning there was a layer of dew around the camp. When the dew was gone, thin flakes like frost on the ground appeared on the desert floor. When the Israelites saw it, they said to each other, "What is it?" For they did not know what it was.

Moses said to them, "It is the bread the LORD has given you to eat."

Exodus 16:12-15
Value: Thankfulness

The Ten Commandments

And God spoke all these words:
"You shall have no other gods before me.
You shall not make for yourself an idol….
You shall not misuse
the name of the LORD….
Remember the Sabbath day
by keeping it holy….
Honor your father and your mother….
You shall not murder.
You shall not commit adultery.
You shall not steal.
You shall not give false testimony….
You shall not covet
your neighbor's house…."

Exodus 20:1, 3-17
Value: Obedience

Ruth Honors Naomi

In the days when the judges ruled, there was a famine in the land. …
And Ruth the Moabitess said to Naomi, "Let me go to the fields and pick up the leftover grain behind anyone in whose eyes I find favor."
Naomi said to her, "Go ahead, my daughter." So she went out and began to glean in the fields behind the harvesters. … So Ruth gleaned in the field until evening. …She carried it back to town, and her mother-in-law saw how much she had gathered. Ruth also brought out and gave her what she had left over after she had eaten enough.

Ruth 1:1, 2:2, 3, 17,18
Value: Respectfulness

Samuel Listens to God

The Lord called Samuel a third time, and Samuel got up and went to Eli and said, "Here I am; you called me."

Then Eli realized that the LORD was calling the boy. So Eli told Samuel, "Go and lie down, and if he calls you, say, 'Speak, LORD, for your servant is listening.'" So Samuel went and lay down in his place.

The LORD came and stood there, calling as at the other times, "Samuel! Samuel!"

Then Samuel said, "Speak, for your servant is listening."

The LORD was with Samuel as he grew up, and he let none of his words fall to the ground.

I Samuel 3:8-10, 19
Value: Responsibility

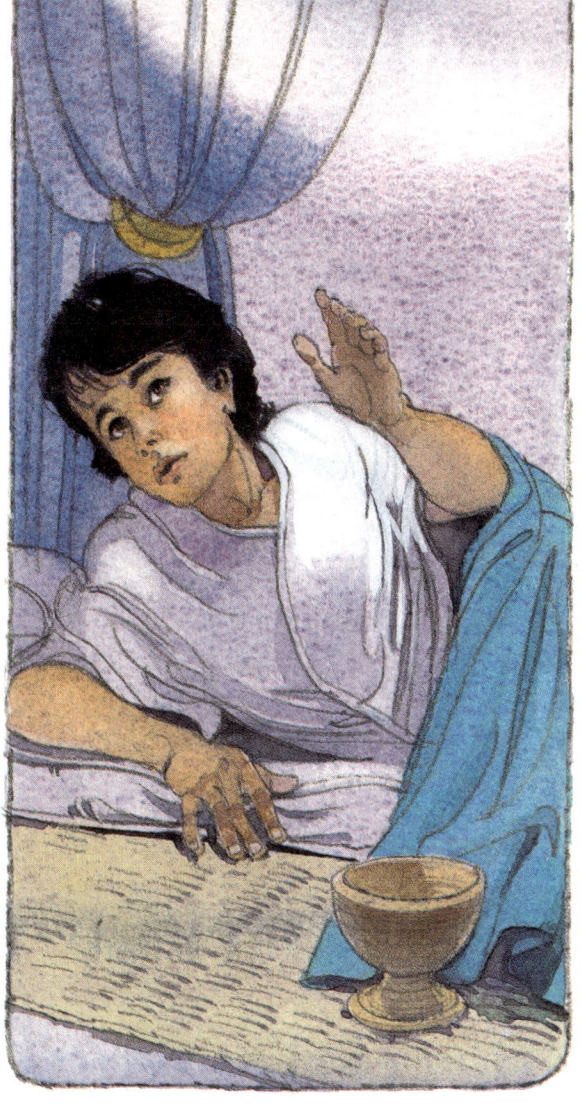

God Chooses David

Jesse had seven of his sons pass before Samuel, but Samuel said to him, "The Lord has not chosen these." So he asked Jesse, "Are these all the sons you have?"
"There is still the youngest," Jesse answered, "but he is tending the sheep." Samuel said, "Send for him; we will not sit down until he arrives."

So he sent and had him brought in. He was ruddy, with a fine appearance and handsome features.

Then the Lord said, "Rise and anoint him; he is the one."

…from that day on the Spirit of the Lord came upon David in power.

I Samuel 16:10-13
Value: Confidence

David and Goliath

As [Goliath] moved closer to attack him, David ran quickly toward the battle line to meet him. Reaching into his bag and taking out a stone, he slung it and struck the Philistine on the forehead. The stone sank into his forehead, and he fell facedown on the ground.

So David triumphed over the Philistine with a sling and a stone; without a sword in his hand he struck down the Philistine and killed him.

I Samuel 17:48-50
Value: Faith

Jonathan Helps David

Then Jonathan said to David: …"The day after tomorrow, toward evening, go to the place where you hid when this trouble began, and wait by the stone Ezel. I will shoot three arrows to the side of it, as though I were shooting at a target. Then I will send a boy and say, 'Go, find the arrows.' If I say to him, 'Look, the arrows are on this side of you; bring them here,' then come, because, as surely as the LORD lives, you are safe; there is no danger. But if I say to the boy, 'Look, the arrows are beyond you,' then you must go, because the LORD has sent you away."

I Samuel 20:18-22
Value: Loyalty

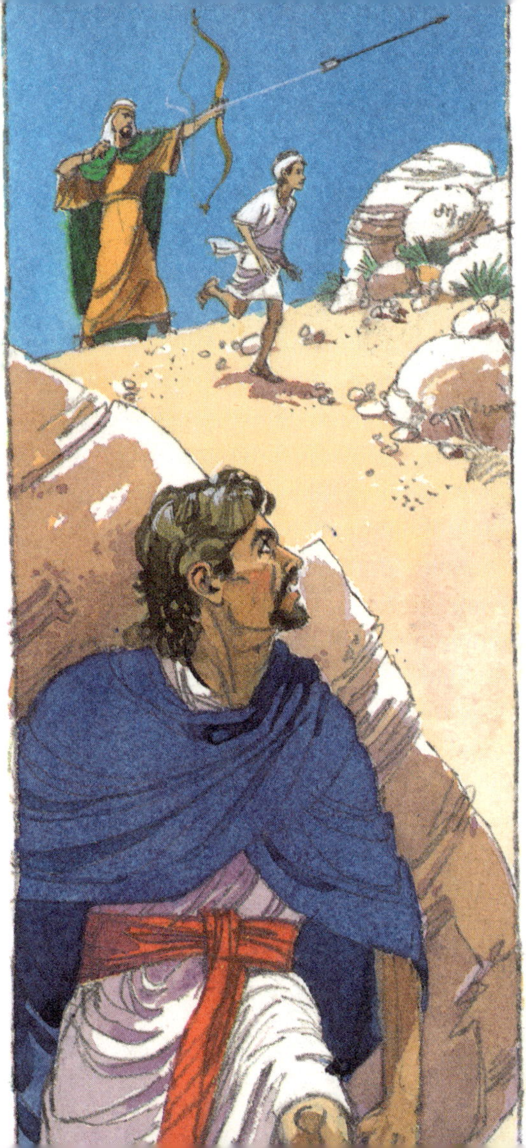

God Guides Elijah

Now Elijah… said to Ahab, "As the LORD, the God of Israel, lives, whom I serve, there will be neither dew nor rain in the next few years except at my word."
Then the word of the LORD came to Elijah: "Leave here, turn eastward and hide in the Kerith Ravine, east of the Jordan. You will drink from the brook, and I have ordered the ravens to feed you there."
So he did what the LORD had told him.
…The ravens brought him bread and meat in the morning and bread and meat in the evening, and he drank from the brook.

I Kings 17:1-6
Value: Faith

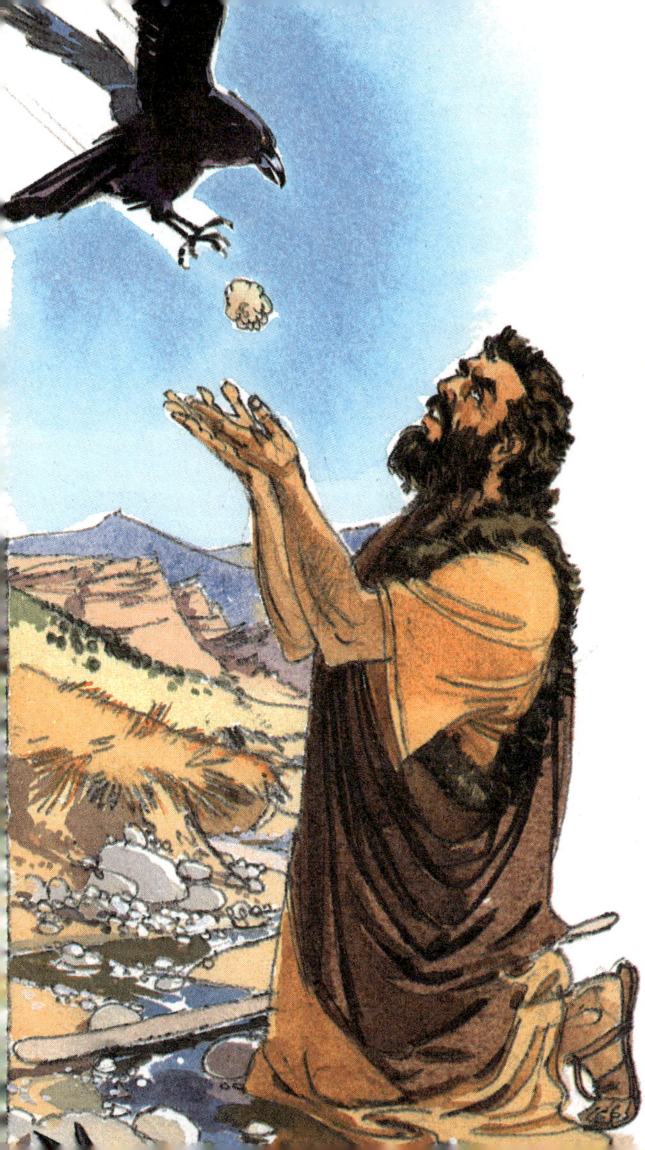

Elijah Goes to Heaven

When the LORD was about to take Elijah up to heaven in a whirlwind, Elijah and Elisha were on their way from Gilgal.
As they were walking along and talking together, suddenly a chariot of fire and horses of fire appeared and separated the two of them, and Elijah went up to heaven in a whirlwind. Elisha saw this and cried out, "My father! My father! The chariots and horsemen of Israel!" And Elisha saw him no more.

II Kings 2:1, 11, 12
Value: Faith

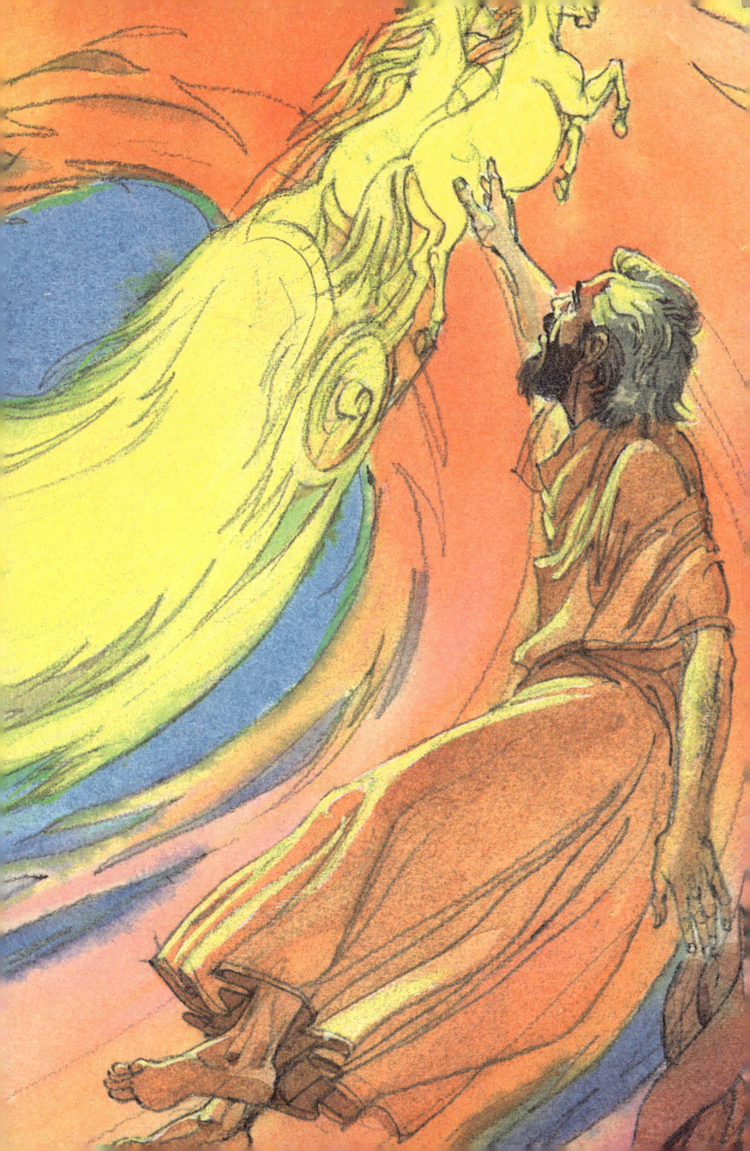

A Servant Girl Helps Naaman

She said to her mistress, "If only my master would see the prophet who is in Samaria! He would cure him of his leprosy."

So Naaman went with his horses and chariots and stopped at the door of Elisha's house. Elisha sent a messenger to say to him, "Go, wash yourself seven times in the Jordan, and your flesh will be restored and you will be cleansed."

So he went down and dipped himself in the Jordan seven times, as the man of God had told him, and his flesh was restored and became clean like that of a young boy.

II Kings 5:3, 9, 10, 14
Value: Helpfulness

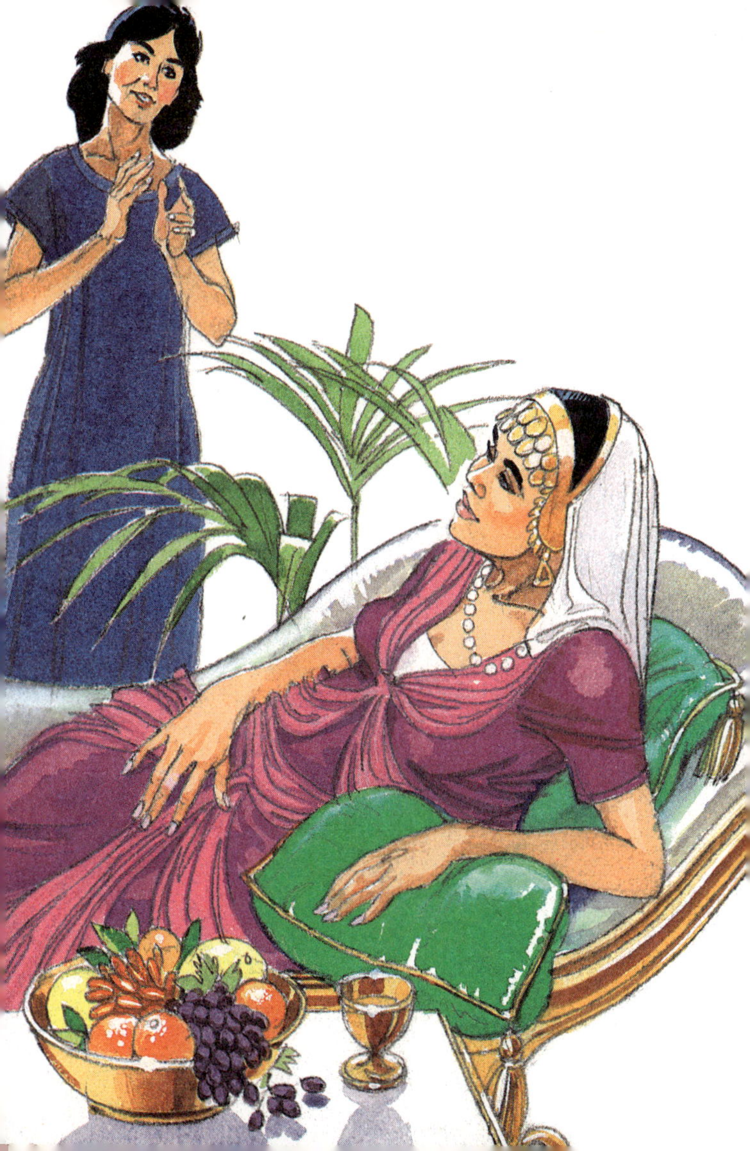

A Fiery Furnace

Nebuchadnezzar then approached the opening of the blazing furnace and shouted, "Shadrach, Meshach and Abednego, servants of the Most High God, come out! Come here!"

So Shadrach, Meshach and Abednego came out of the fire, and the satraps, prefects, governors and royal advisers crowded around them. They saw that the fire had not harmed their bodies, nor was a hair of their heads singed; their robes were not scorched, and there was no smell of fire on them.

Daniel 3:26, 27
Value: Obedience

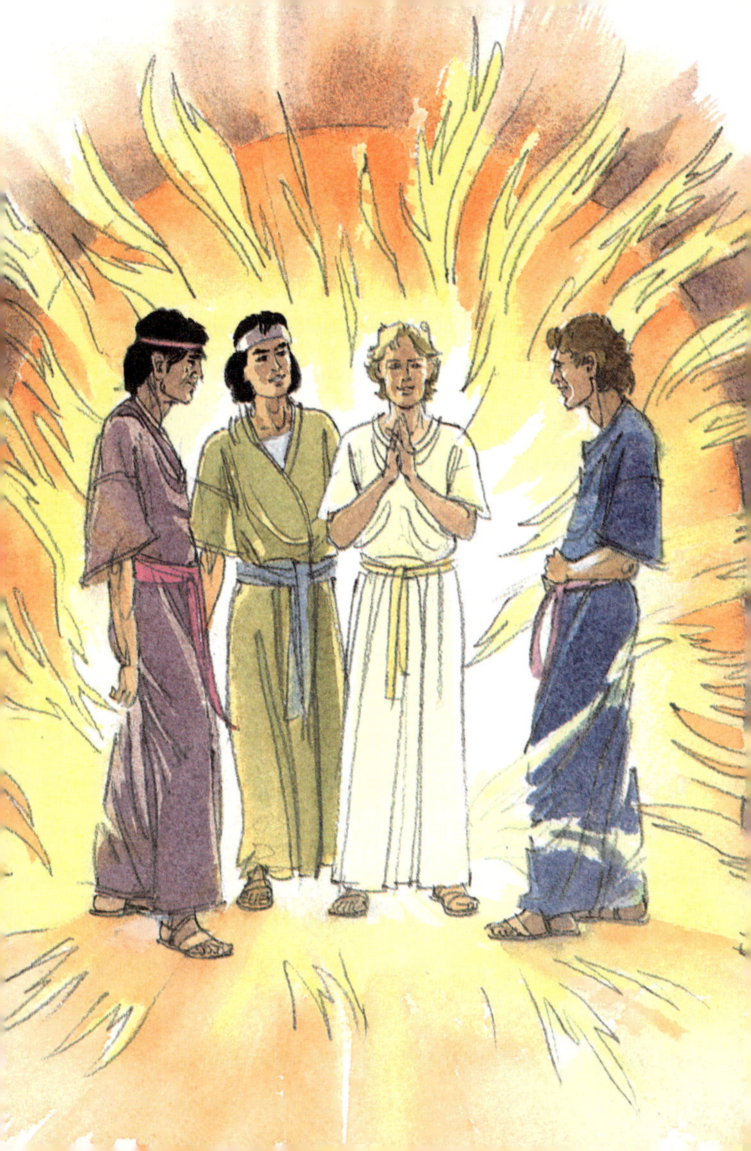

Daniel and the Lions

So the king gave the order, and they brought Daniel and threw him into the lions' den....

Then the king returned to his palace and spent the night without eating and without any entertainment being brought to him. And he could not sleep.

At the first light of dawn, the king got up and hurried to the lions' den. When he came near the den, he called to Daniel in an anguished voice, "Daniel, servant of the living God, has your God, whom you serve continually, been able to rescue you from the lions?"

Daniel answered, "O king, live forever! My God sent his angel, and he shut the mouths of the lions."

Daniel 6:16, 18-22
Value: Courage

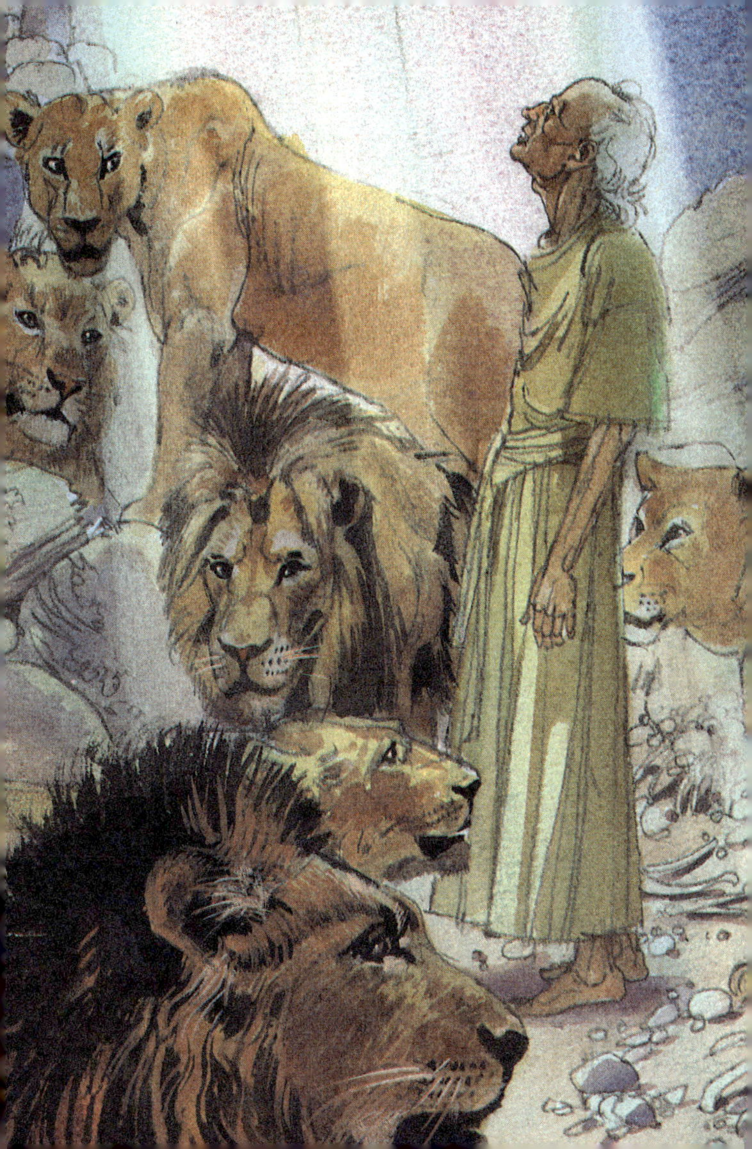

Jonah and the Big Fish

Then the LORD sent a great wind on the sea, and such a violent storm arose that the ship threatened to break up.

The sea was getting rougher and rougher. So they asked him [Jonah], "What should we do to you to make the sea calm down for us?"

"Pick me up and throw me into the sea," he replied, "and it will become calm. I know that it is my fault that this great storm has come upon you."

Then they took Jonah and threw him overboard, and the raging sea grew calm. But the LORD provided a great fish to swallow Jonah, and Jonah was inside the fish three days and three nights.

Jonah 1:4, 11, 12, 15, 17
Value: Obedience

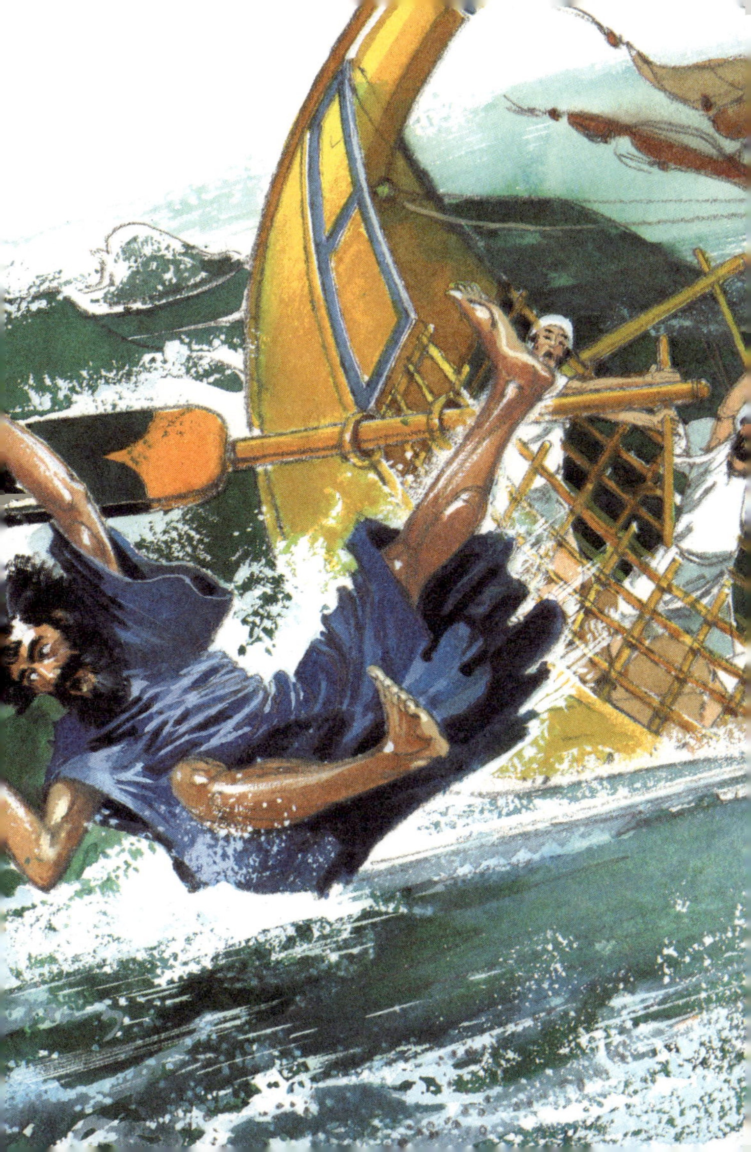

Mary Hears a Promise

…The virgin's name was Mary. The angel went to her and said, "Greetings, you who are highly favored! The LORD is with you." Mary was greatly troubled at his words and wondered what kind of greeting this might be. But the angel said to her, "Do not be afraid, Mary, you have found favor with God. You will be with child and give birth to a son, and you are to give him the name Jesus. He will be great and will be called the Son of the Most High. The LORD God will give him the throne of his father David, and he will reign over the house of Jacob forever; his kingdom will never end."

Luke 1:27-33
Value: Joyfulness

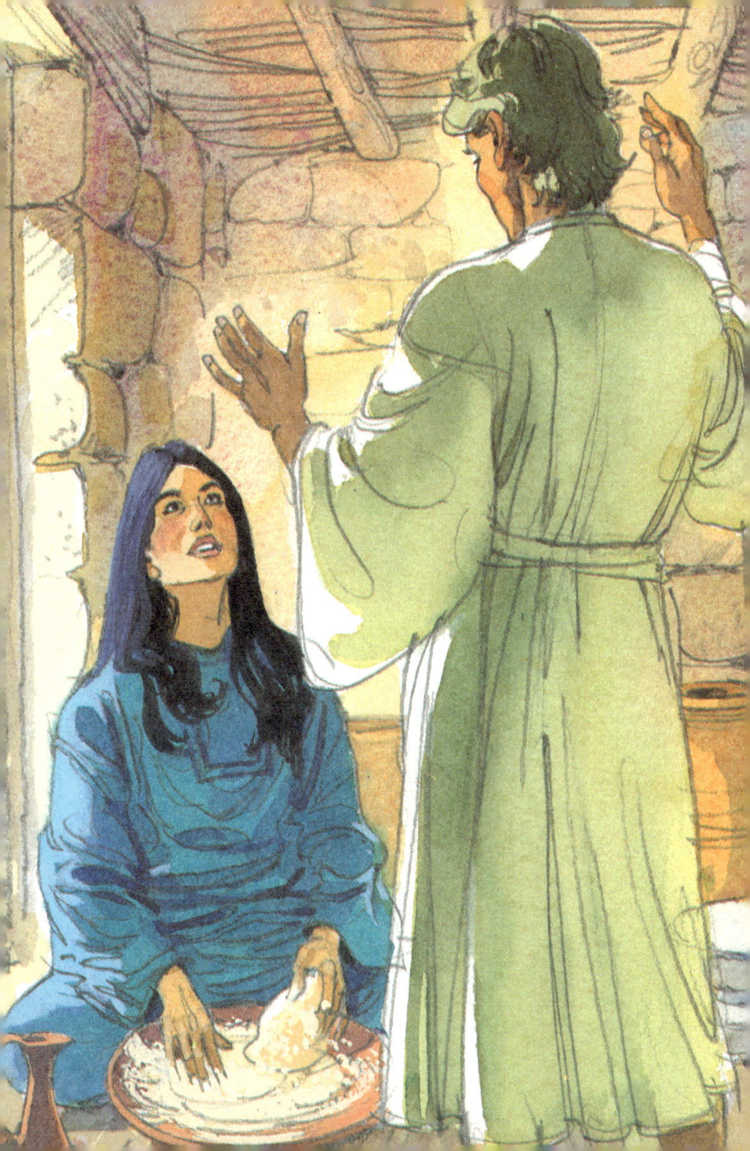

Wise Men Rejoice

After Jesus was born in Bethlehem in Judea, during the time of King Herod, Magi from the east came to Jerusalem and asked, "Where is the one who has been born king of the Jews? We saw his star in the east and have come to worship him."

On coming to the house, they saw the child with his mother Mary, and they bowed down and worshiped him. Then they opened their treasures and presented him with gifts of gold and of incense and of myrrh.

Matthew 2:1, 2, 11
Value: Joyfulness

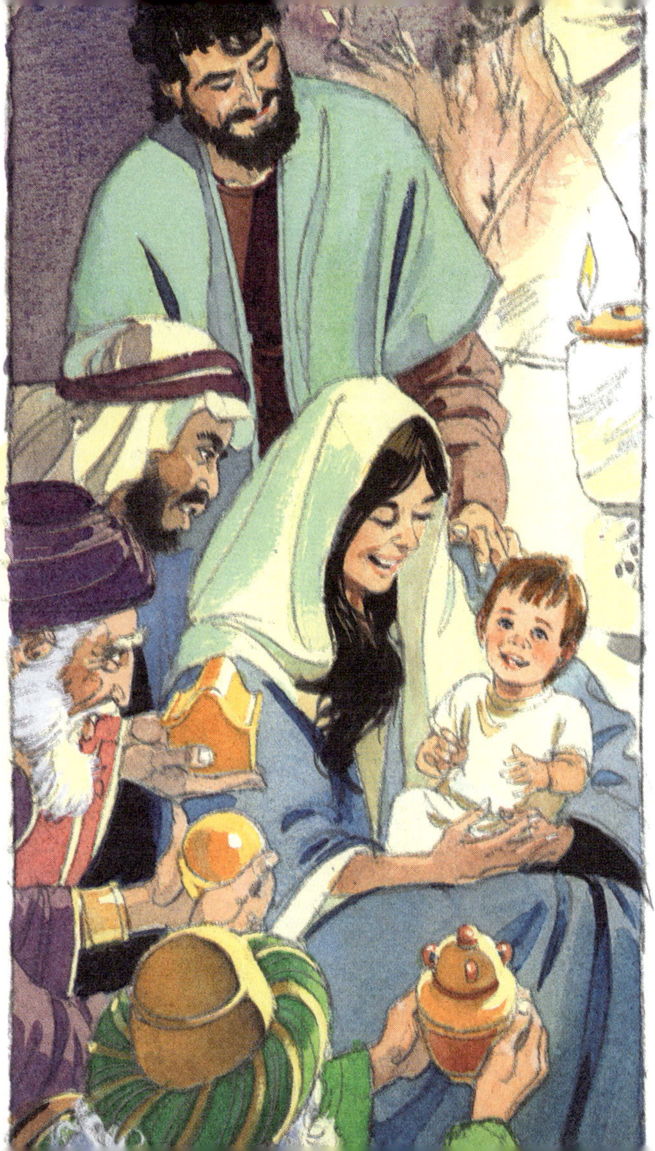

Fishers of Men

When [Jesus] had finished speaking, he said to Simon, "Put out into deep water, and let down the nets for a catch."
Simon answered, "Master we've worked hard all night and haven't caught anything. But because you say so, I will let down the nets."
When they had done so, they caught such a large number of fish that their nets began to break.
…he and all his companions were astonished at the catch of fish they had taken, and so were James and John, the sons of Zebedee, Simon's partners.
Then Jesus said to Simon, "Don't be afraid; from now on you will catch men."
So they pulled their boats up on shore, left everything and followed him.

Luke 5:4-6, 9-11
Value: Helpfulness

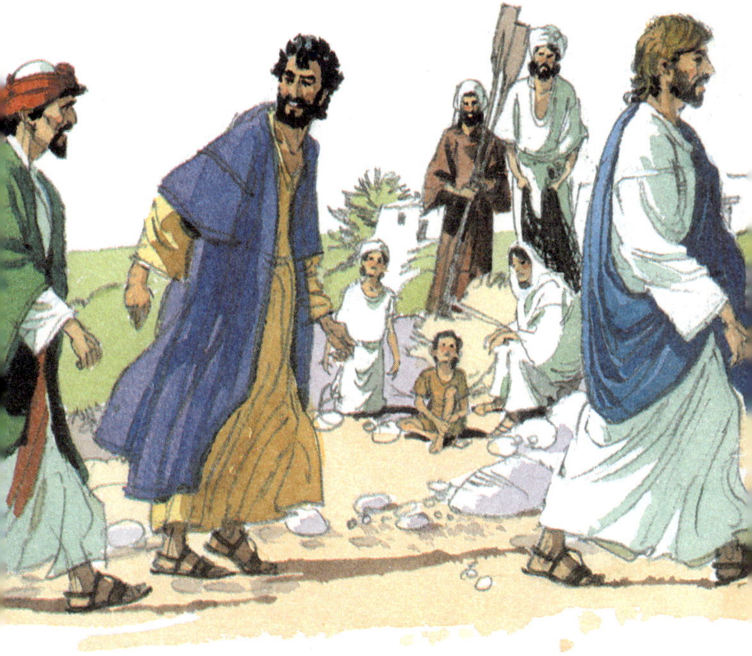

The Lord's Prayer

"This is how you should pray:
"'Our Father in heaven,
hallowed be your name,
your kingdom come,
your will be done
   on earth as it is in heaven.
Give us today our daily bread.
Forgive us our debts,
   as we also have forgiven our debtors.
And lead us not into temptation,
but deliver us from the evil one.'"

Matthew 6:9-13
Value: Prayerfulness

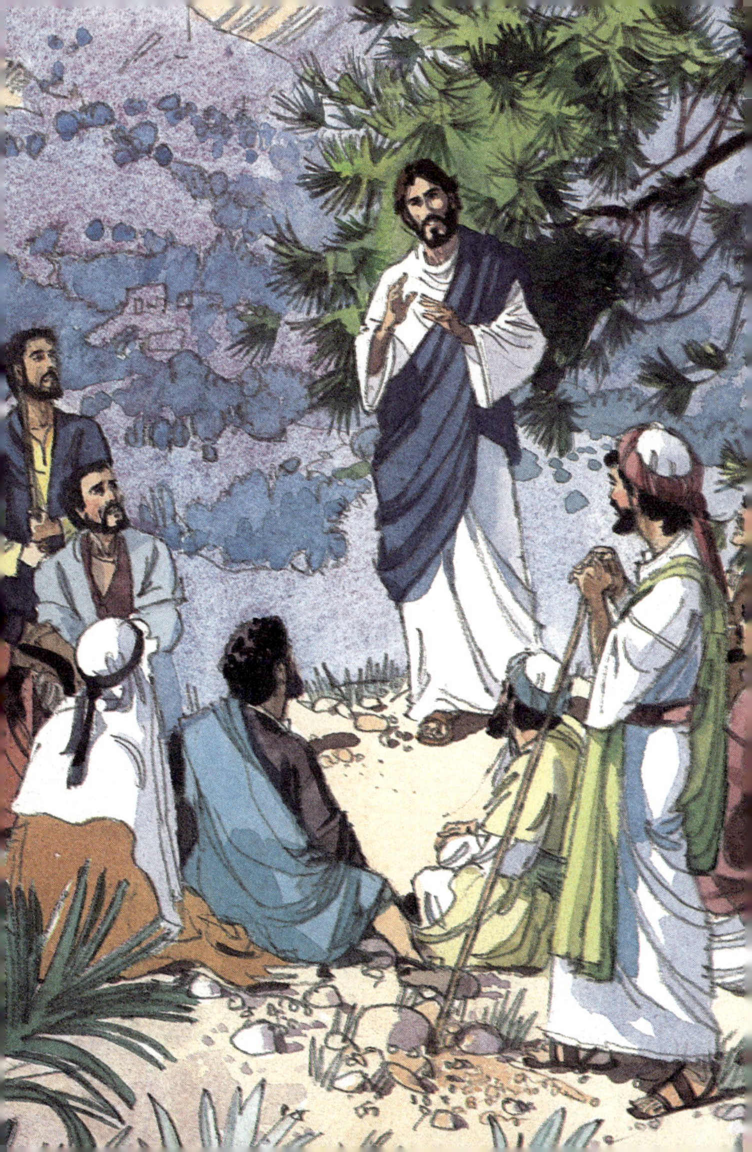

Calming a Storm

A furious squall came up, and the waves broke over the boat, so that it was nearly swamped. Jesus was in the stern, sleeping on a cushion. The disciples woke him and said to him, "Teacher, don't you care if we drown?"

He got up, rebuked the wind and said to the waves, "Quiet! Be still!" Then the wind died down and it was completely calm.

He said to his disciples, "Why are you so afraid? Do you still have no faith?"

They were terrified and asked each other, "Who is this? Even the wind and the waves obey him!"

Mark 4:37-41
Value: Courage

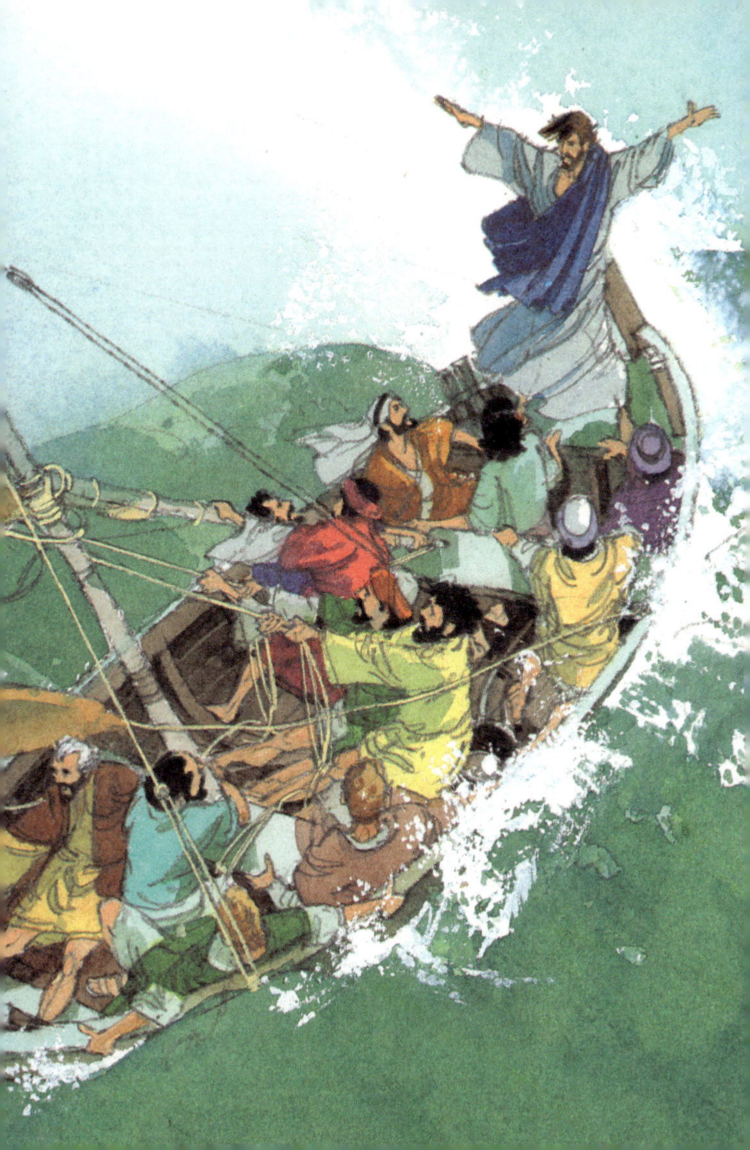

Jesus Heals a Deaf Man

There some people brought a man to him who was deaf and could hardly talk, and they begged him to place his hand on the man.

After he took him aside, away from the crowd, Jesus put his fingers into the man's ears. Then he spit and touched the man's tongue. He looked up to heaven and with a deep sigh said to him, *"Ephphatha!"* (which means "Be opened!"). At this, the man's ears were opened, his tongue was loosened and he began to speak plainly. People were overwhelmed with amazement.

Mark 7:32, 35, 37
Value: Compassion

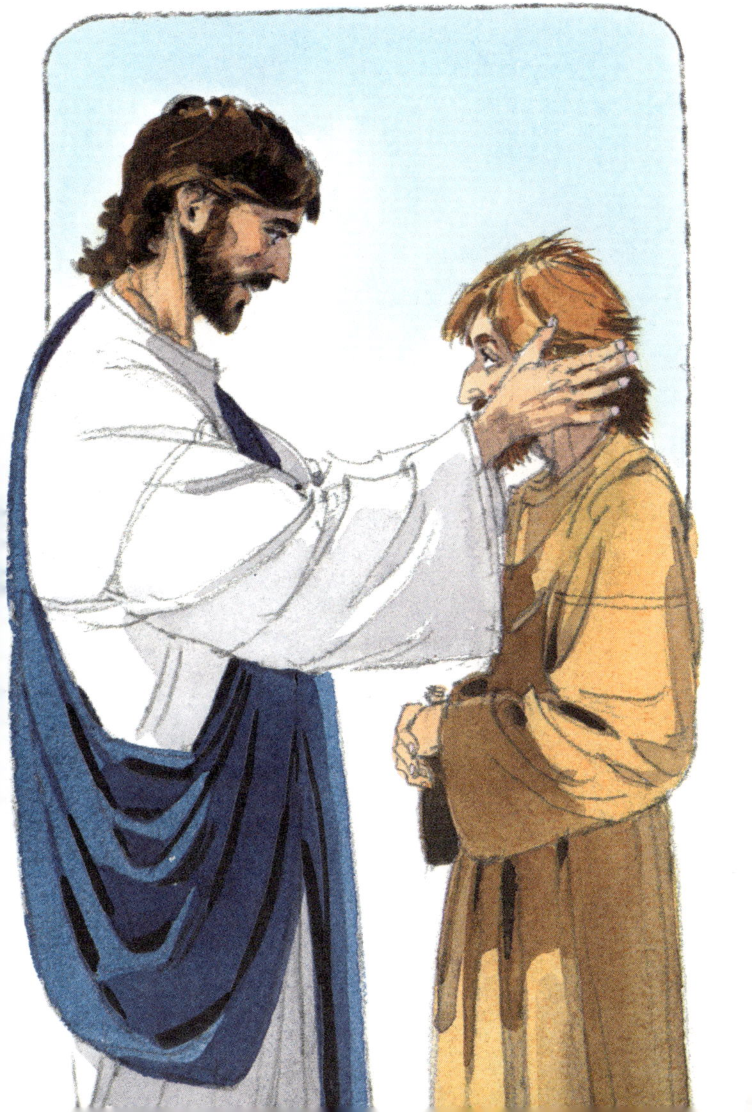

Jesus Is Our Best Friend

People were bringing little children to Jesus to have him touch them. ... He said to them, "Let the little children come to me, and do not hinder them, for the kingdom of God belongs to such as these. I tell you the truth, anyone who will not receive the kingdom of God like a little child will never enter it." And he took the children in his arms, put his hands on them and blessed them.

Mark 10:13-16
Value: Faith

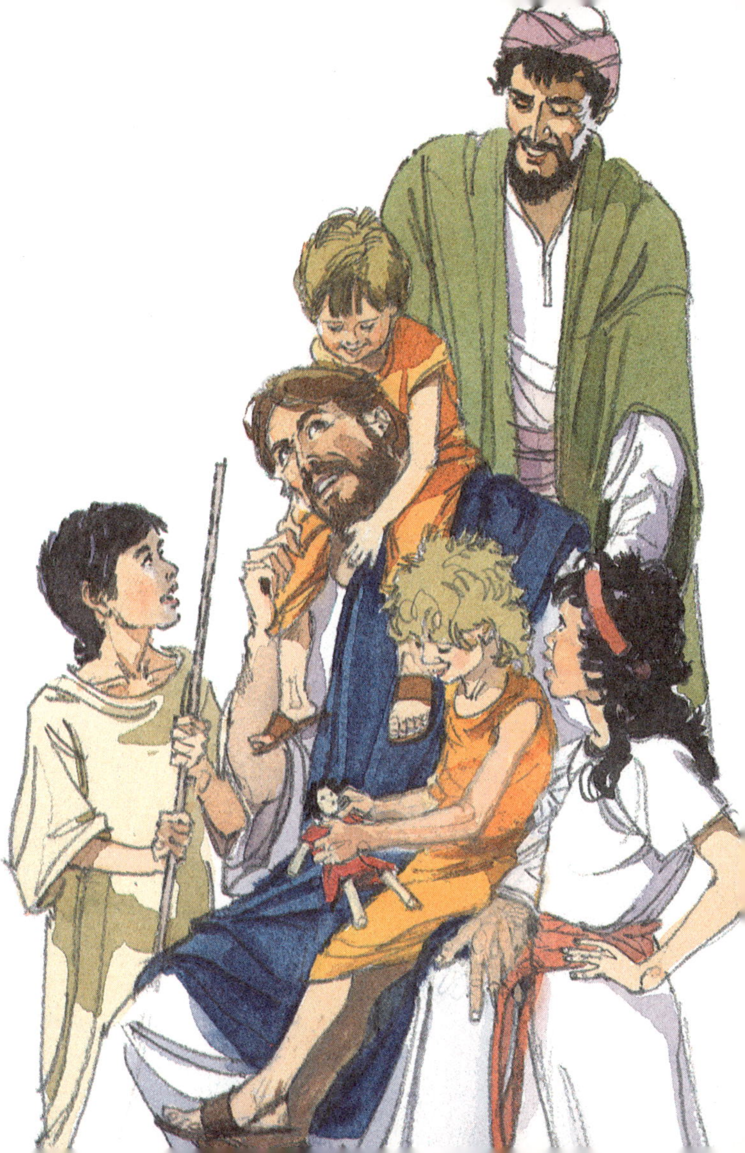

The Good Samaritan

..."A man was going down from Jerusalem to Jericho, when he fell into the hands of robbers. They stripped him of his clothes, beat him and went away, leaving him half dead.

"But a Samaritan, as he traveled, came where the man was; and when he saw him, he took pity on him. He went to him and bandaged his wounds, pouring on oil and wine. Then he put the man on his own donkey, took him to an inn and took care of him."

Luke 10:30, 33, 34
Value: Compassion

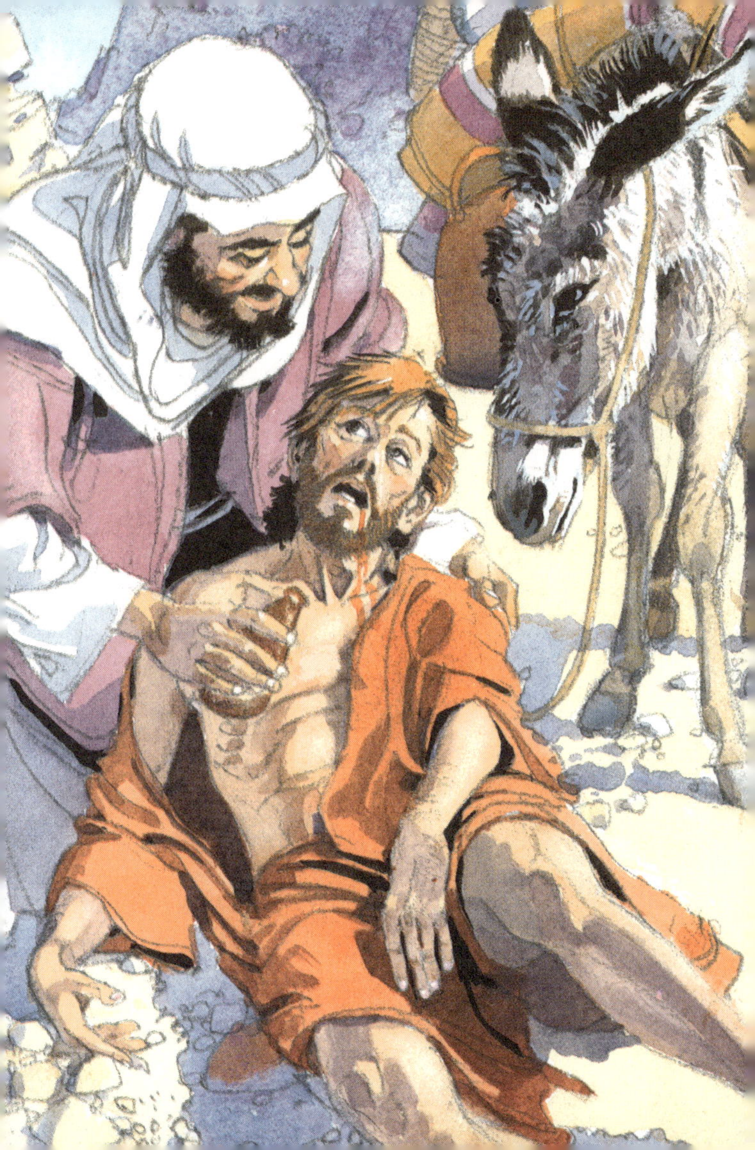

Zacchaeus Is Sorry

He wanted to see who Jesus was, but being a short man he could not, because of the crowd. So he ran ahead and climbed a sycamore-fig tree to see him, since Jesus was coming that way.

When Jesus reached the spot, he looked up and said to him, "Zacchaeus, come down immediately. I must stay at your house today."

Zacchaeus stood up and said to the Lord, "Look, Lord! Here and now I give half of my possessions to the poor, and if I have cheated anybody out of anything, I will pay back four times the amount."

Luke 19:3-5, 8
Value: Stewardship

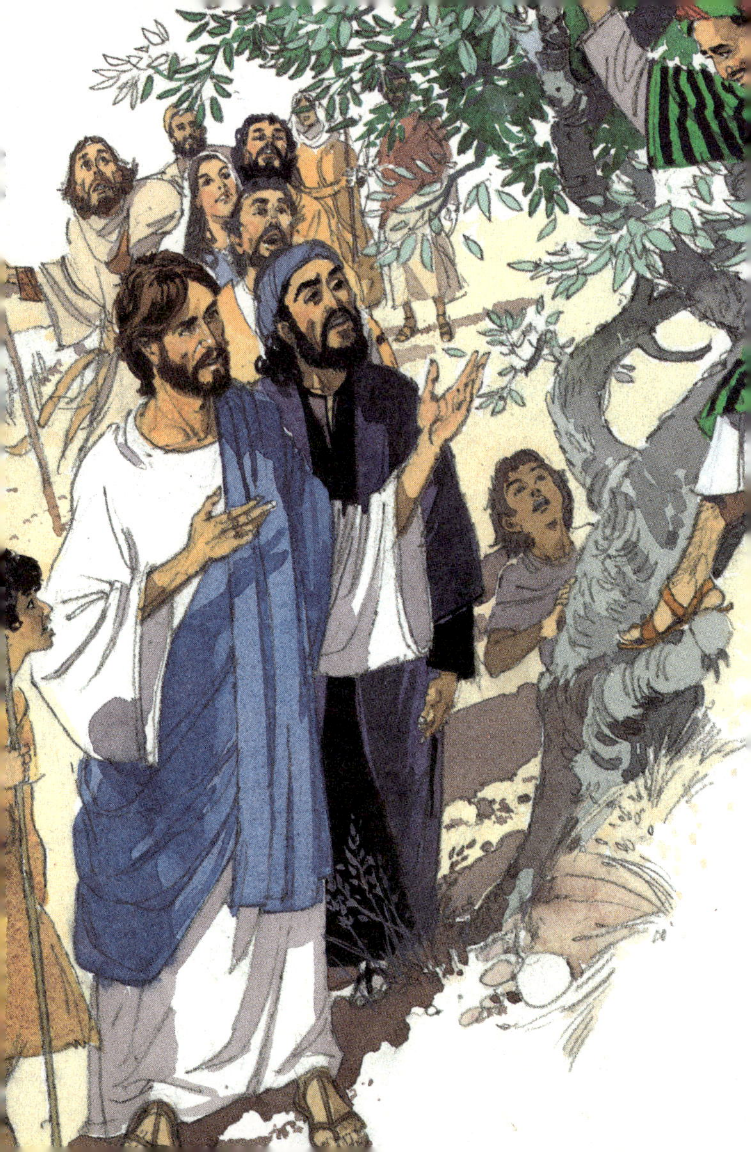

Feeding 5,000

… Andrew, Simon Peter's brother, spoke up, "Here is a boy with five small barley loaves and two small fish, but how far will they go among so many?"

Jesus said, "Have the people sit down."… Jesus then took the loaves, gave thanks, and distributed to those who were seated as much as they wanted. He did the same with the fish.

When they had all had enough to eat, he said to his disciples, "Gather the pieces that are left over. Let nothing be wasted." So they gathered them and filled twelve baskets with the pieces of the five barley loaves left over by those who had eaten.

John 6:8-13
Value: Resourcefulness

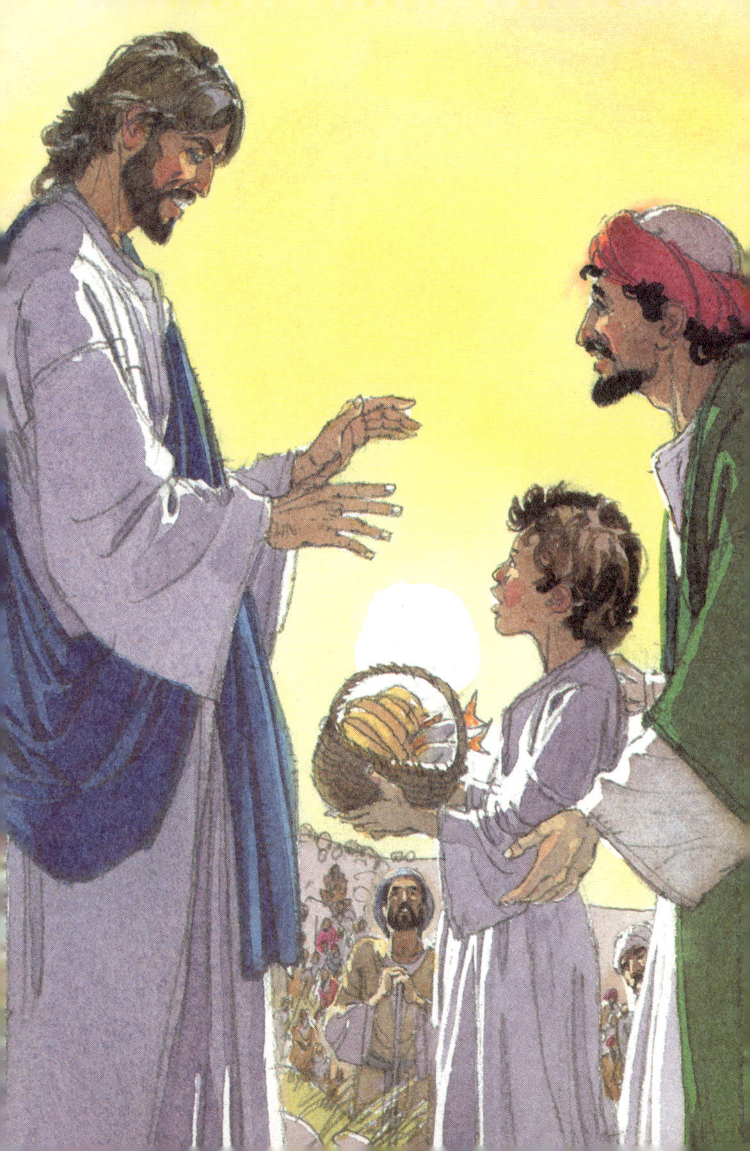

Lazarus Comes Back to Life

On his arrival, Jesus found that Lazarus had already been in the tomb for four days.

"Lord," Martha said to Jesus, "if you had been here, my brother would not have died. But I know that even now God will give you whatever you ask."

Jesus said to her, "Your brother will rise again."

...Jesus called in a loud voice, "Lazarus, come out!" The dead man came out, his hands and feet wrapped with strips of linen, and a cloth around his face.

Jesus said to them, "Take off the grave clothes and let him go."

John 11:17, 21-23, 43, 44
Value: Compassion

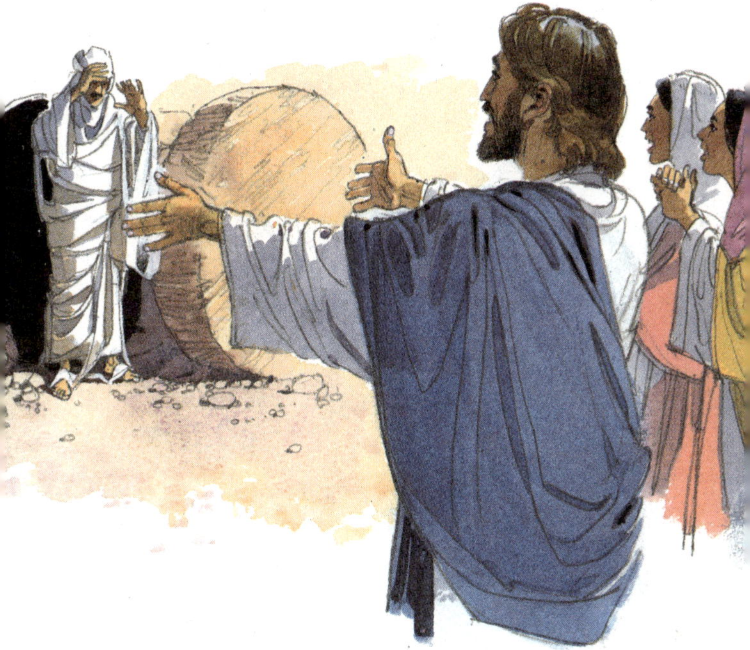

Jesus, the King and Savior

"Go to the village ahead of you, and as you enter it, you will find a colt tied there, which no one has ever ridden. Untie it and bring it here. If anyone asks you, 'Why are you untying it?' tell him, 'The Lord needs it.'"

Those who were sent ahead went and found it just as he had told them. As they were untying the colt, its owners asked them, "Why are you untying the colt?" They replied, "The Lord needs it."

As he went along, people spread their cloaks on the road. ... the whole crowd of disciples began joyfully to praise God in loud voices for all the miracles they had seen.

Luke 19:30-34, 36, 37
Value: Praise

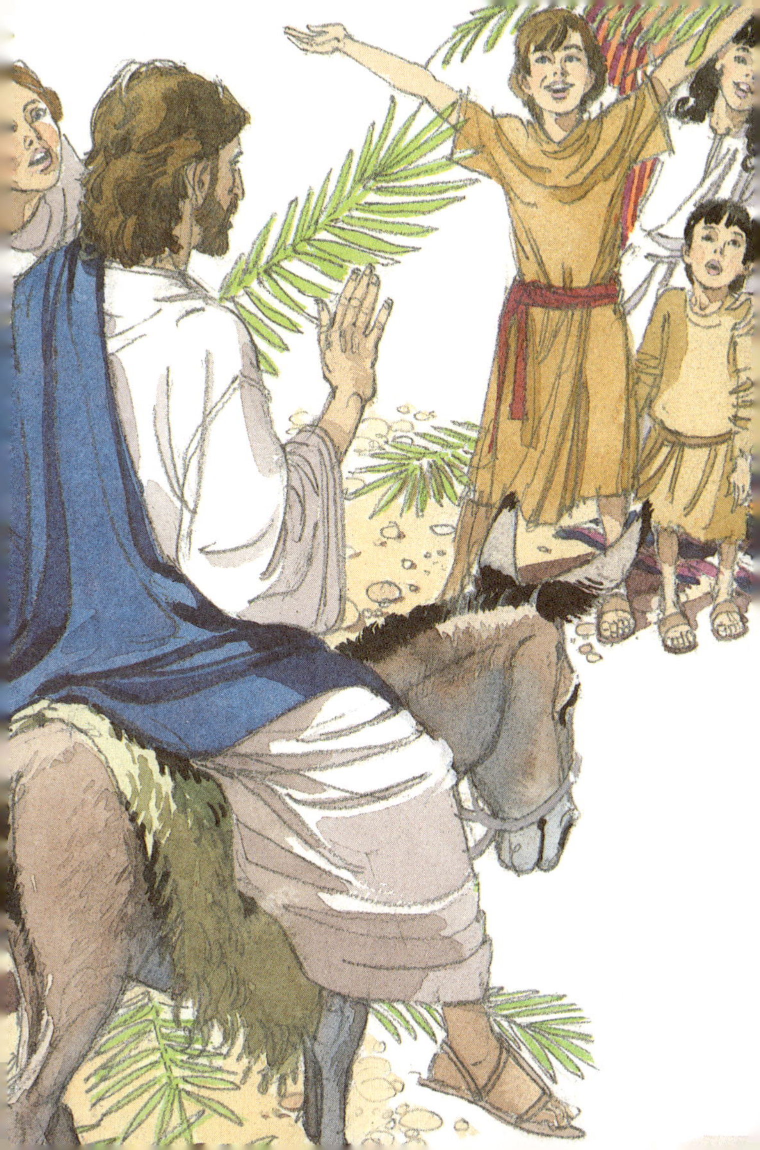

Jesus Says Good-Bye

As the Father has loved me, so have I loved you. Now remain in my love. If you obey my commands, you will remain in my love, just as I have obeyed my Father's commands and remain in his love.
I came from the Father and entered the world; now I am leaving the world and going back to the Father.
I have told you these things, so that in me you may have peace. In this world you will have trouble. But take heart! I have overcome the world.

John 15:9, 10; 16:28, 33
Value: Courage

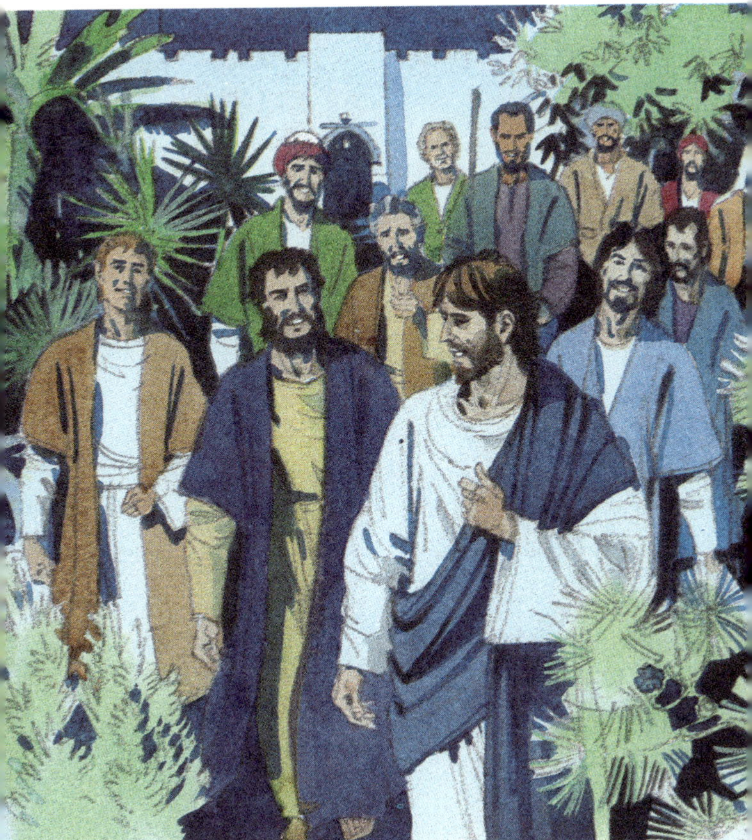

Jesus Dies for Us

Wanting to release Jesus, Pilate appealed to [the crowd] again. But they kept shouting, "Crucify him! Crucify him!" When they came to the place called The Skull, there they crucified him, along with the criminals—one on his right, the other on his left. Jesus said, "Father, forgive them, for they do not know what they are doing." And they divided up his clothes by casting lots.

It was now about the sixth hour, and darkness came over the whole land until the ninth hour.

Jesus called out with a loud voice, "Father, into your hands I commit my spirit." When he had said this, he breathed his last.

Luke 23:20, 21, 33, 34, 44, 46
Value: Forgiveness

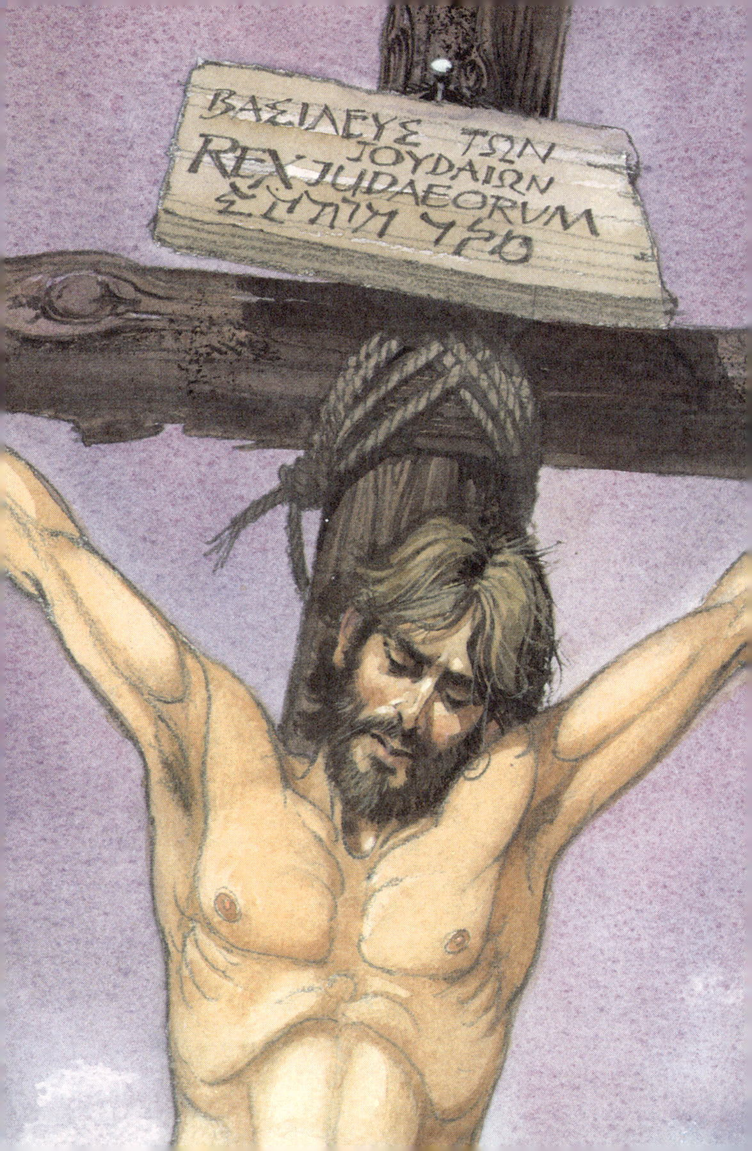
ΒΑΣΙΛΕΥΣ ΤΩΝ
ΙΟΥΔΑΙΩΝ
REX JUDAEORUM

Mary and an Empty Tomb

Early on the first day of the week, while it was still dark, Mary of Magdala went to the tomb and saw that the stone had been removed from the entrance.
…she turned around and saw Jesus standing there, but she did not realize it was Jesus.
"Woman," he said, "why are you crying? Who is it you are looking for?"
Thinking he was the gardener, she said, "Sir, if you have carried him away, tell me where you have put him, and I will get him."
Jesus said to her, "Mary."
She turned to him and cried out… "Teacher."

John 20:1, 14-16
Value: Joyfulness

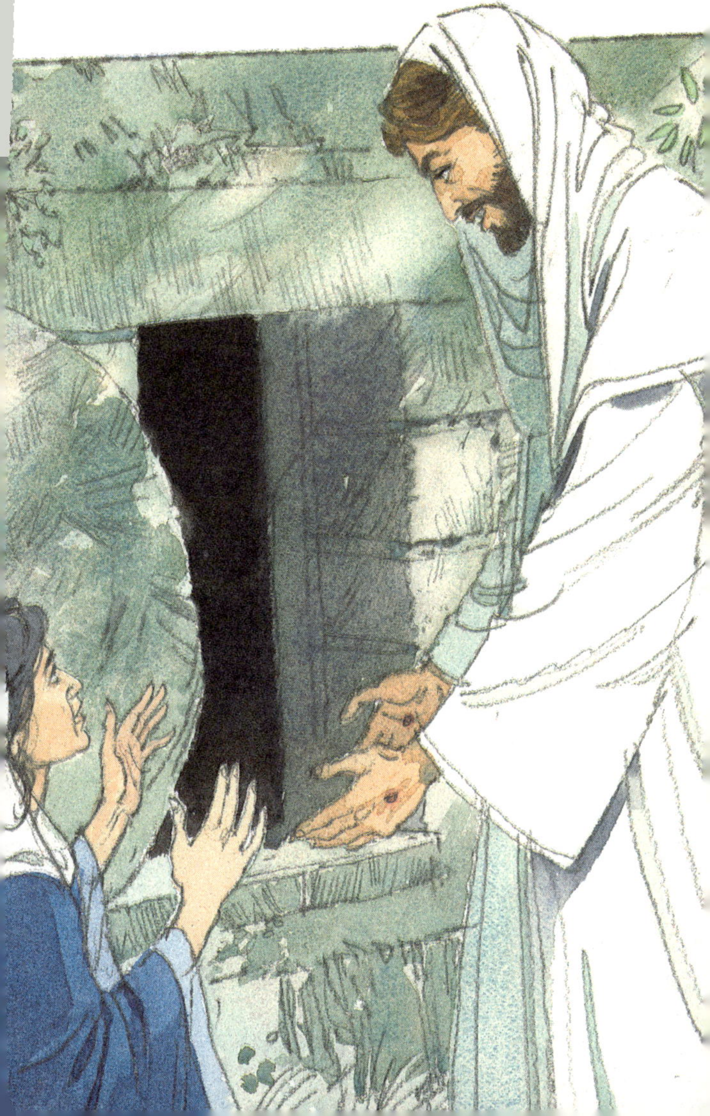

Not Alone

While they [the disciples] were still talking about this, Jesus himself stood among them and said to them, "Peace be with you."

They were startled and frightened, thinking they saw a ghost. He said to them, "Why are you troubled, and why do doubts rise in your minds? Look at my hands and my feet. It is I myself! Touch me and see; a ghost does not have flesh and bones, as you see I have."

…The disciples were overjoyed when they saw the Lord.

And with that he breathed on them and said, "Receive the Holy Spirit. If you forgive anyone his sins, they are forgiven; if you do not forgive them, they are not forgiven."

Luke 24:36-39; John 20:20, 22, 23
Value: Joyfulness

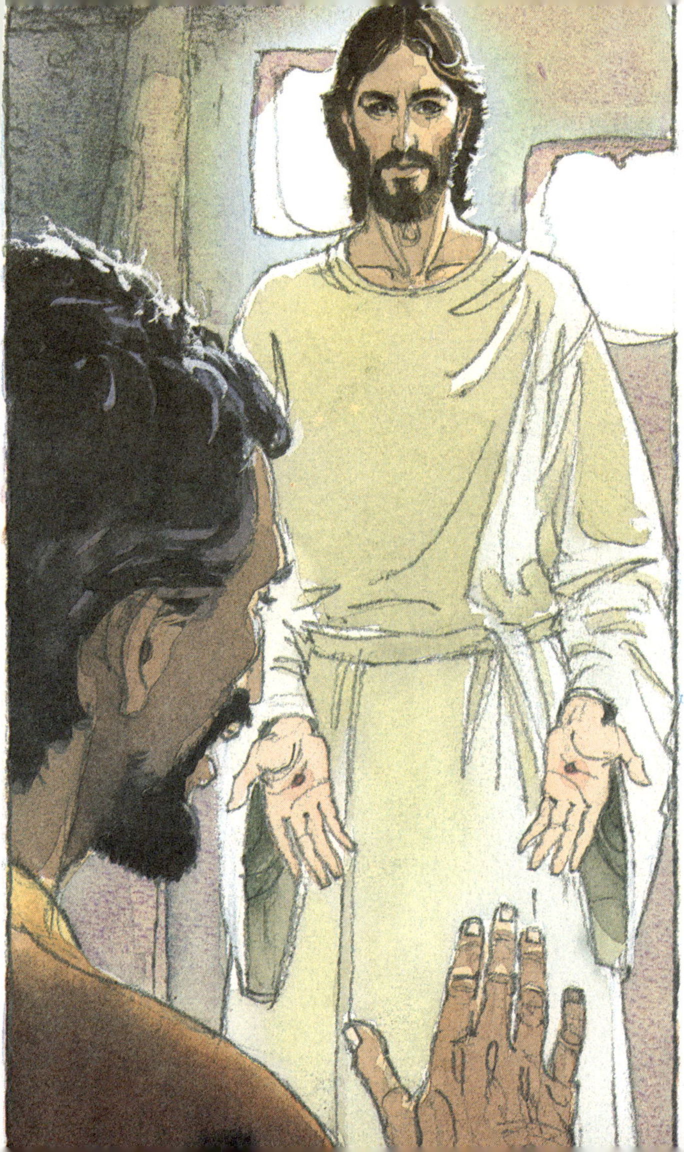

Jesus Goes to Heaven

"But you will receive power when the Holy Spirit comes on you; and you will be my witnesses in Jerusalem, and in all Judea and Samaria, and to the ends of the earth."

After he said this, he was taken up before their very eyes, and a cloud hid him from their sight.

They were looking intently up into the sky as he was going, when suddenly two men dressed in white stood beside them. "Men of Galilee," they said, "why do you stand here looking into the sky? This same Jesus, who has been taken from you into heaven, will come back in the same way you have seen him go into heaven."

Acts 1:8-11
Value: Forgiveness

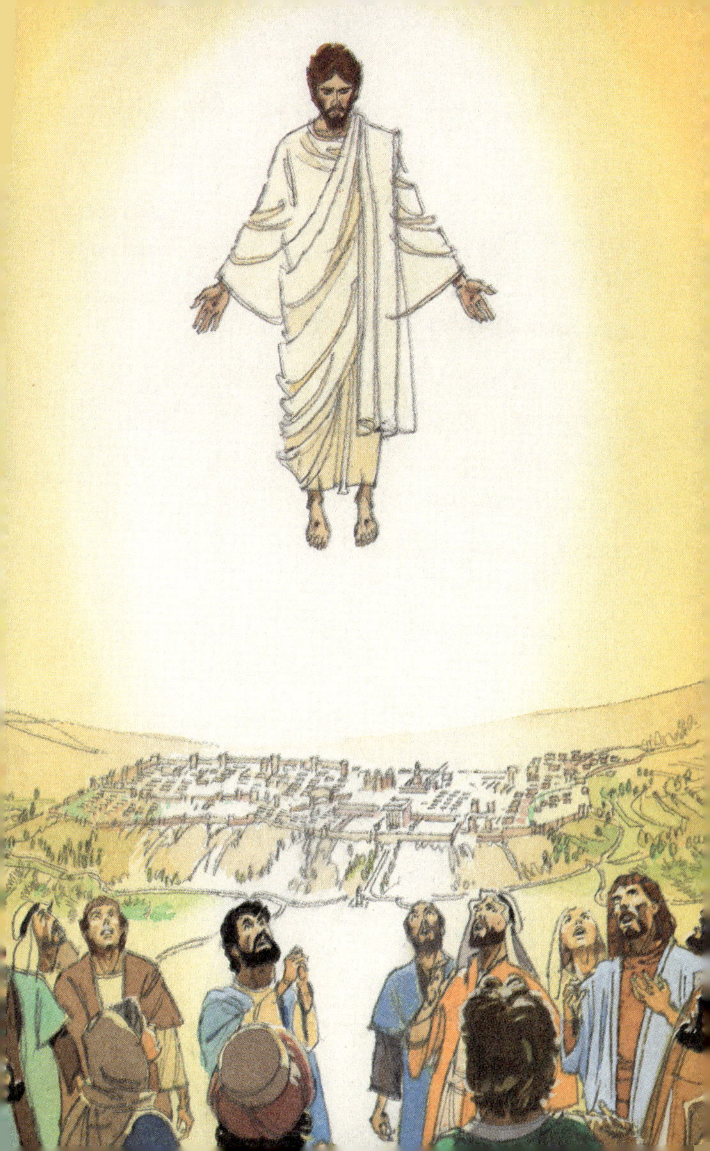

God Rescues Peter

The night before Herod was to bring him to trial, Peter was sleeping between two soldiers, bound with two chains, and sentries stood guard at the entrance. Suddenly an angel of the Lord appeared and a light shone in the cell. He struck Peter on the side and woke him up. "Quick, get up!" he said, and the chains fell off Peter's wrists.

Then the angel said to him, "Put on your clothes and sandals." And Peter did so. "Wrap your cloak around you and follow me," the angel told him. Peter followed him out of the prison.

Acts 12:6-9
Value: Faith

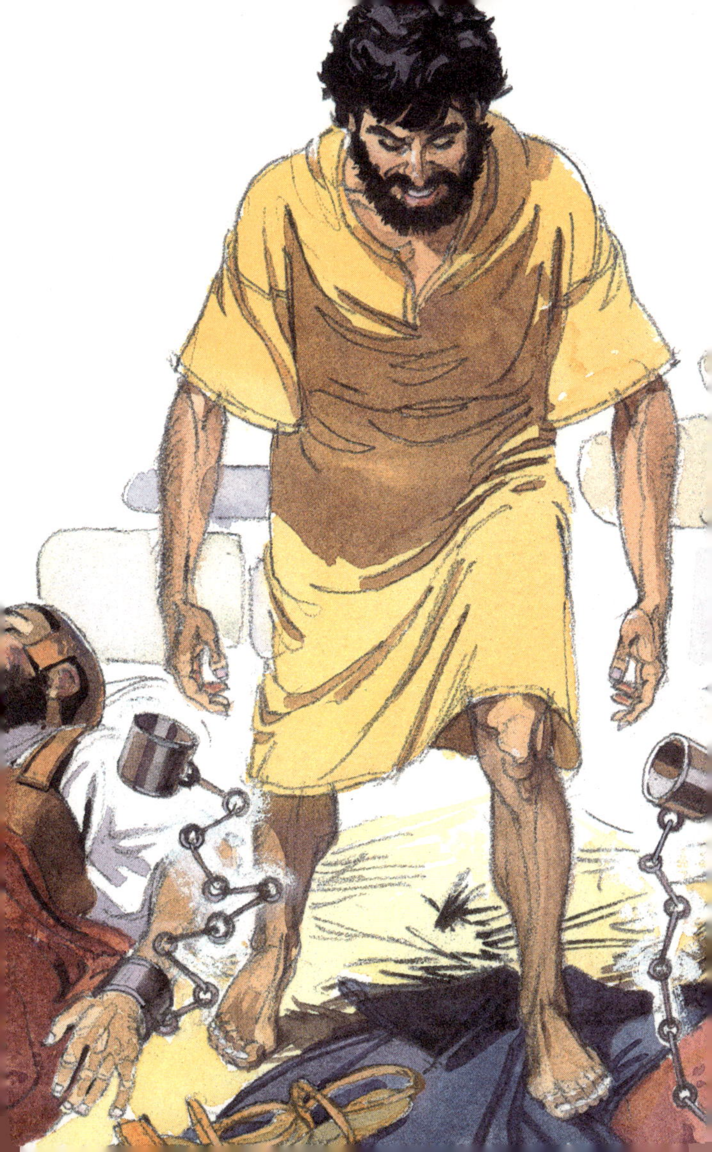

A Miracle and a Mistake

...Paul looked directly at him, saw that he had faith to be healed and called out, "Stand up on your feet!" At that, the man jumped up and began to walk.

When the crowd saw what Paul had done, they shouted in the Lycaonian language, "The gods have come down to us in human form!"

But when the apostles Barnabas and Paul heard of this, they tore their clothes and rushed out into the crowd, shouting: "Men, why are you doing this? We too are only men, human like you. We are bringing you good news, telling you to turn from these worthless things to the living God, who made heaven and earth and sea and everything in them."

Acts 14:9-11, 14, 15
Value: Faith

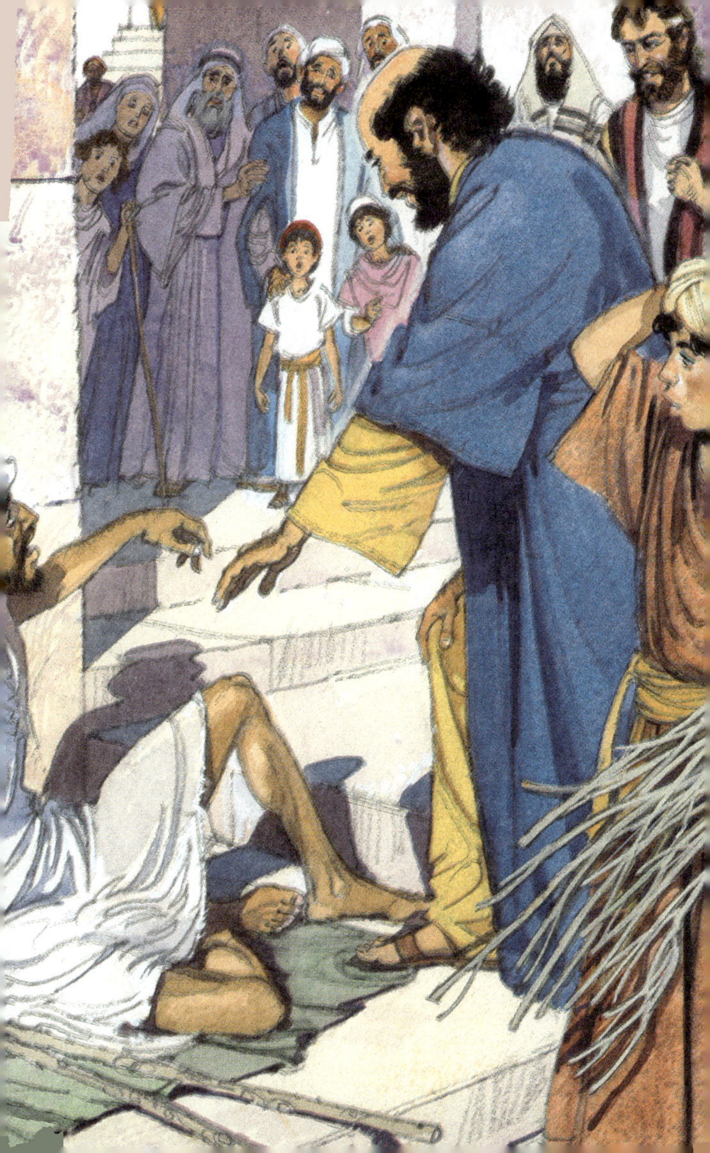

Paul Helps a Church

Every Sabbath he reasoned in the synagogue, trying to persuade Jews and Greeks.
When Silas and Timothy came from Macedonia, Paul devoted himself exclusively to preaching, testifying to the Jews that Jesus was the Christ. But when the Jews opposed Paul and became abusive, he shook out his clothes in protest....
One night the Lord spoke to Paul in a vision: "Do not be afraid; keep on speaking, do not be silent."...
So Paul stayed for a year and a half, teaching them [the Gentiles] the word of God.

Acts 18:4-6, 9, 11
Value: Conviction

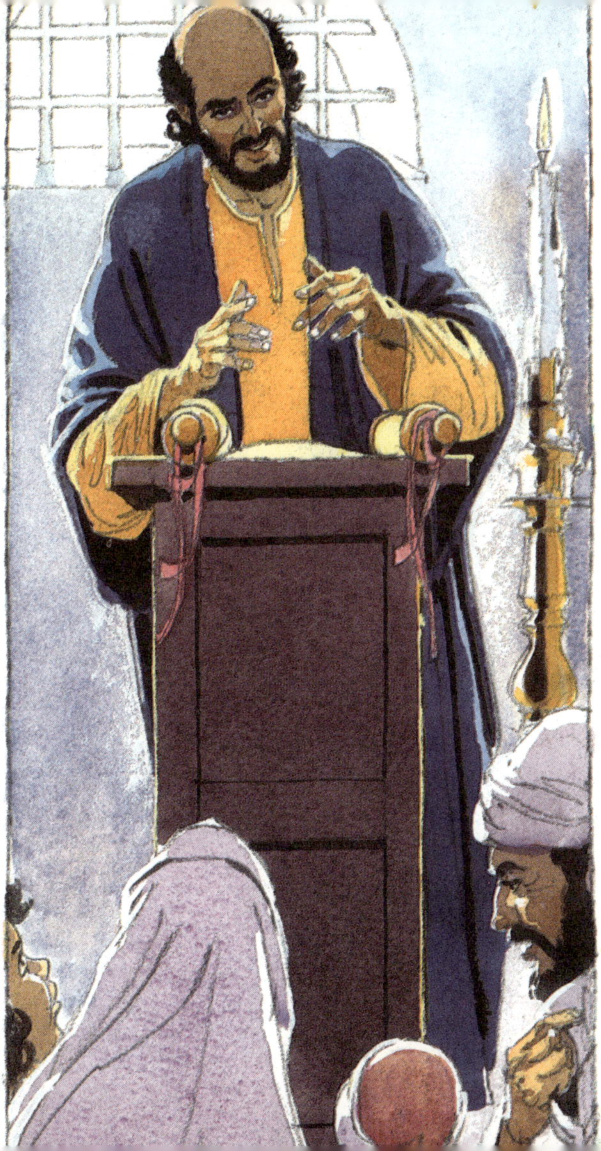

John Writes about God's Love

My dear children, I write this to you so that you will not sin. But if anybody does sin, we have one who speaks to the Father in our defense—Jesus Christ, the Righteous One. He is the atoning sacrifice for our sins, and not only for ours but also for the sins of the whole world.
And now, dear children, continue in him, so that when he appears we may be confident and unashamed before him at his coming.

I John 2:1, 2, 28
Value: Love

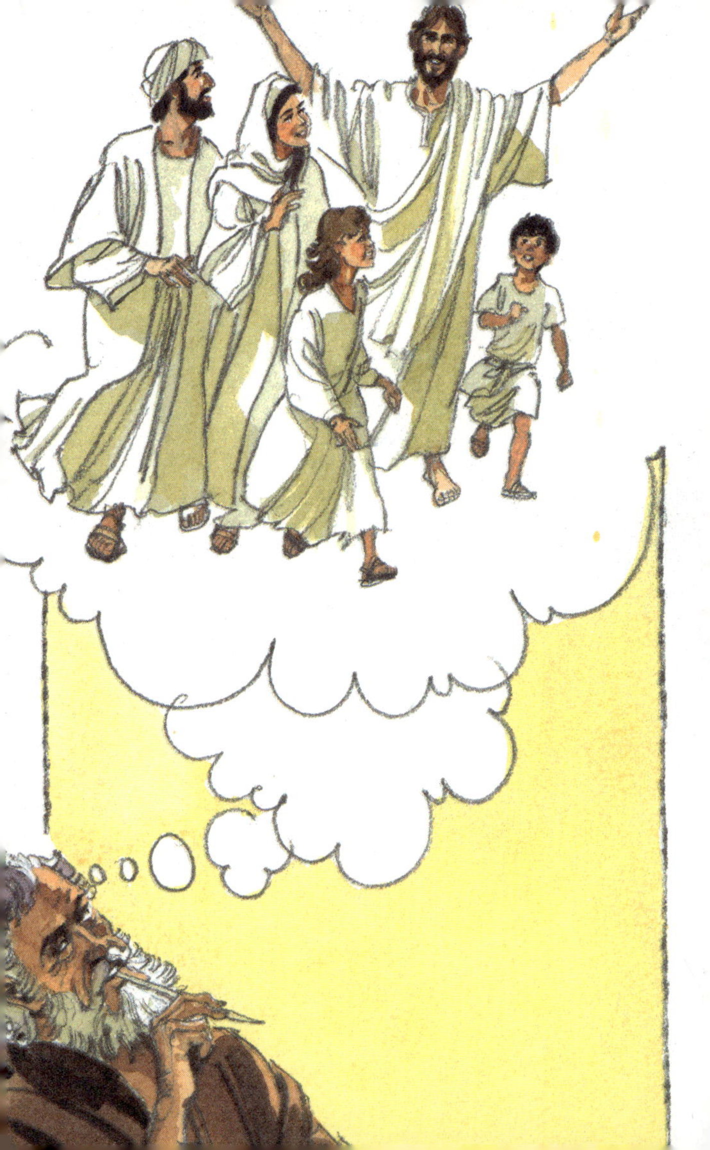

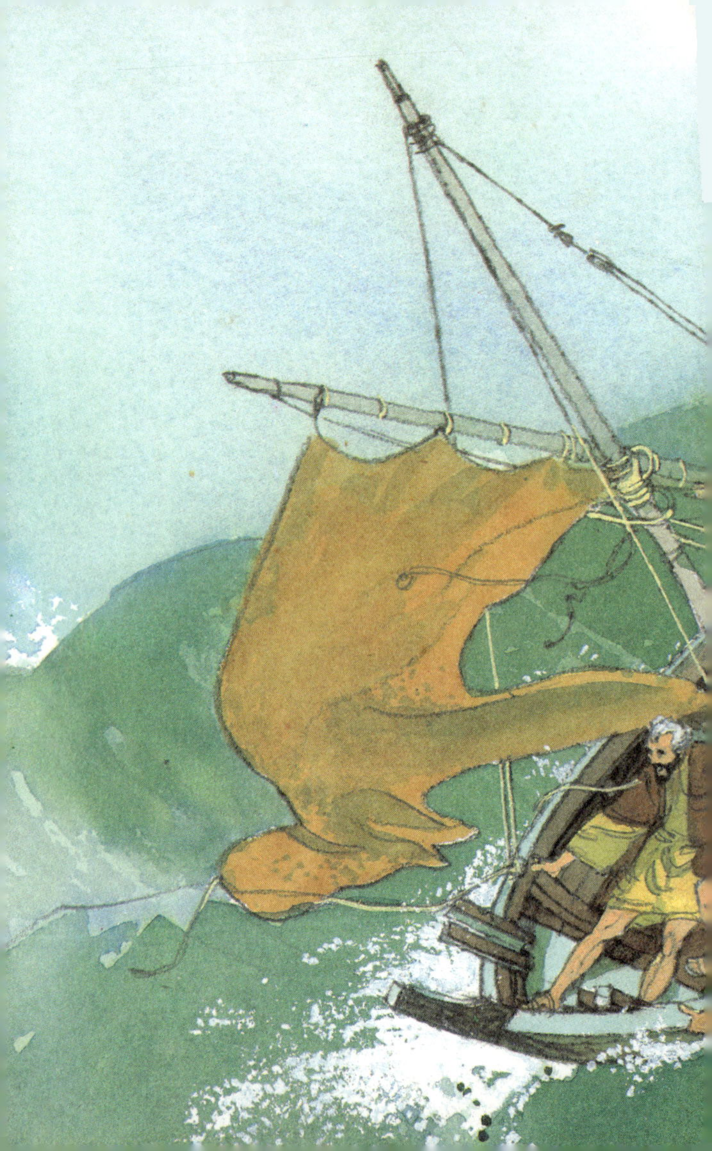